LEVEL 2 SCIENCE

LET'S READ AND FIND OUT

THE MOON SEEMS TO CHANGE

BY FRANKLYN M. BRANLEY

ILLUSTRATED BY BARBARA AND ED EMBERLEY

Revised Edition

HARPER

An Imprint of HarperCollinsPublishers

The Let's-Read-and-Find-Out Science book series was originated by Dr. Franklyn M. Branley, Astronomer Emeritus and former Chairman of the American Museum of Natural History–Hayden Planetarium, and was formerly co-edited by him and Dr. Roma Gans, Professor Emeritus of Childhood Education, Teachers College, Columbia University. Text and illustrations for each of the books in the series are checked for accuracy by an expert in the relevant field. For more information about Let's-Read-and-Find-Out Science books, write to HarperCollins Children's Books, 195 Broadway, New York, NY 10007, or visit our website at www.letsreadandfindout.com.

Let's Read-and-Find-Out Science® is a trademark of HarperCollins Publishers.

Library of Congress Cataloging-in-Publication Data
Branley, Franklyn Mansfield, (date)
    The moon seems to change.
    (Let's-read-and-find-out science book)
    Summary: Explains the phases of the moon—the changes that seem to happen to it as it goes around Earth.
    ISBN 978-0-06-238206-1
    1. Moon—Juvenile literature.   [1. Moon—Phases]   I. Emberley, Barbara, ill.   II. Emberley, Ed, ill.   III. Title.
QB582.B72   1987   86-27097
523.3'2

Photo of full moon on page 27 by Ewen A. Whitaker

15 16 17 18 19   SCP   10 9 8 7 6 5 4 3 2 1
❖
Revised edition, 2015

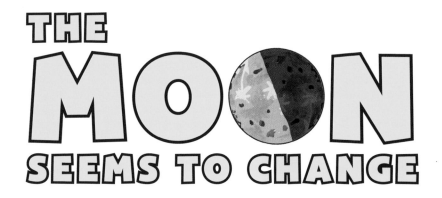

THE MOON
SEEMS TO CHANGE

Tonight take a look at the sky. See if the moon is there.

It may be big and round. It is a full moon.

FULL

Maybe you will see only part of it. It may be a quarter moon.

QUARTER

Or it may be only a little sliver. It is called a crescent moon.

CRESCENT

As the nights go by you can see changes in the moon. After the moon is full you see less and less of it. There are three or four nights with no moon at all. Then you see more and more of it. The moon seems to change.

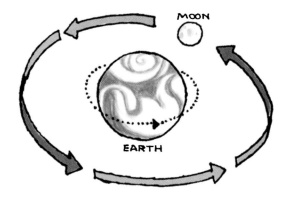

It really doesn't. It seems to change because the moon goes around Earth. As it goes around, we see more of it—the moon gets bigger. It is a waxing moon. Or we see less of it—the moon gets smaller. It is a waning moon.

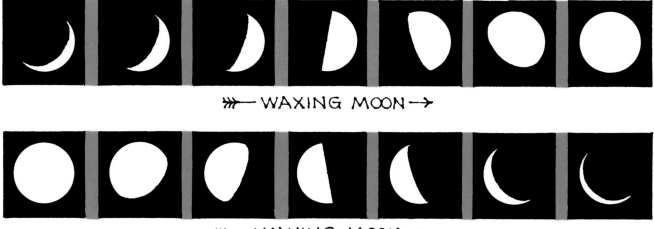

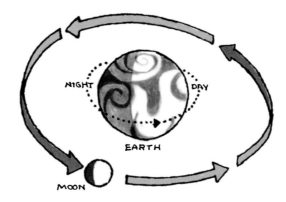

Half of the moon is always lighted by the sun. Half is lighted and half is always in darkness. It's the same with Earth. While one half of Earth is having sunshine and daylight, the other half is getting no sunshine. It is night.

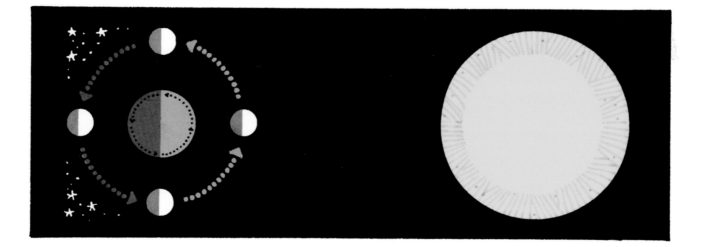

A day on Earth is 24 hours long.

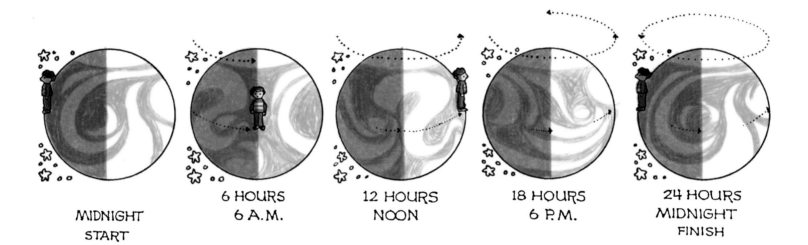

| MIDNIGHT START | 6 HOURS 6 A.M. | 12 HOURS NOON | 18 HOURS 6 P.M. | 24 HOURS MIDNIGHT FINISH |

A day on the moon is almost a month long.

| START | ABOUT 1 WEEK | ABOUT 2 WEEKS | ABOUT 3 WEEKS | ABOUT 4 WEEKS FINISH |

It takes the moon about four weeks to go around Earth.

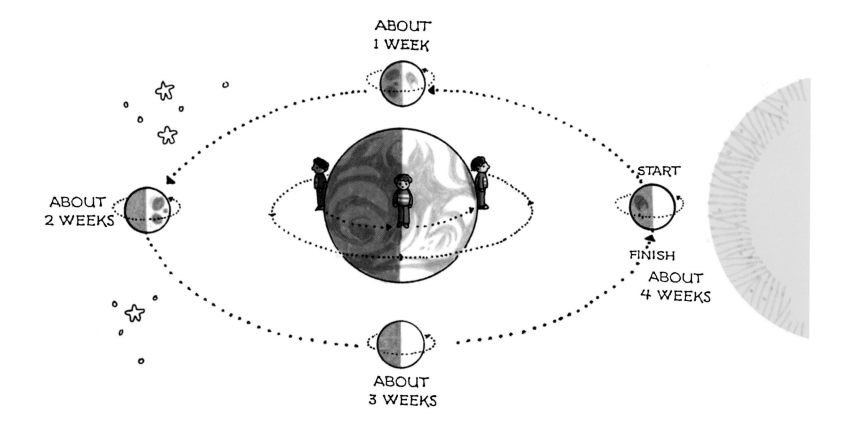

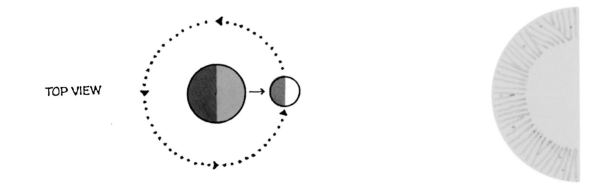

TOP VIEW

As the moon goes around Earth, it is sometimes between Earth and the sun. The dark half of the moon is facing us. We cannot see any of the lighted half. This is called new moon.

DARK SIDE OF MOON FACING US SO WE CANNOT SEE IT.

NEW MOON NOT IN NIGHT SKY SO WE CANNOT SEE IT.

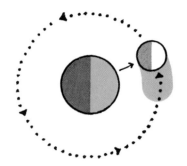

A night or two later the moon has moved a little bit along its path around Earth. We can then see a small part of the lighted half. It is called a crescent moon. We see it just after sunset. It is in the west, where we see the sun go down. You may be able to see it before the sky is dark. Sometimes you can see it in daytime.

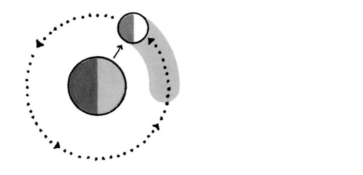

Each night the moon seems to grow. The moon is waxing.
We can see a bit more of the lighted half.

14

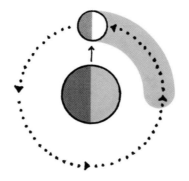

About a week after the moon is new, it has become a first-quarter moon. It looks like this. Sometimes you can see it in the afternoon before the sky is dark.

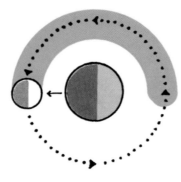 

After another week the moon is on one side of Earth and the sun is on the other side. We can see all the lighted half of the moon. It is a full moon. We see it in the east as the sun sets in the west. We can't see it in the daytime.

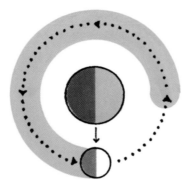 

Each night after it is full, we see less and less of the moon. The moon is waning. In about a week it is a quarter moon. This is third quarter. It can be seen after midnight.

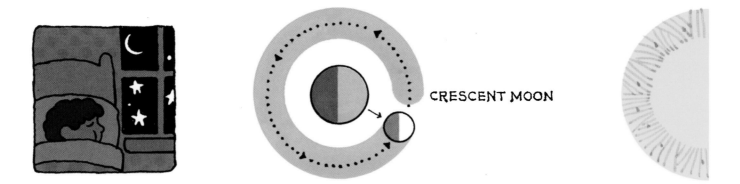

CRESCENT MOON

After that, the moon once more becomes a crescent. Each night the crescent gets a bit thinner. We would see it later and later at night—long after we're usually asleep. A few days later we cannot see the moon at all. It is once again a new moon. About four weeks after the moon is new, we have another new moon.

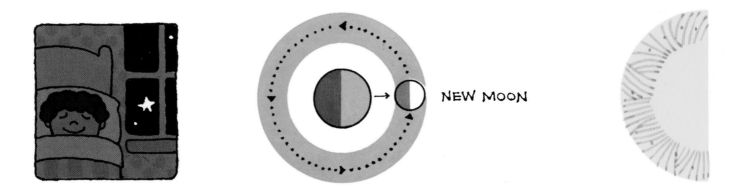

NEW MOON

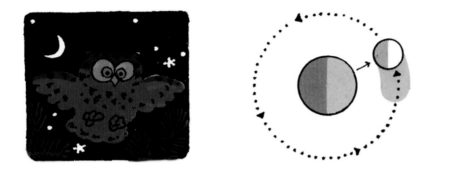 

Two or three nights later, the moon has become a thin crescent. Night after night the same changes occur. Keep watch on the skies and you will see the changes—new moon, crescent, first quarter, full moon, third quarter, crescent, and back to new moon. All together, the changes are called the phases of the moon.

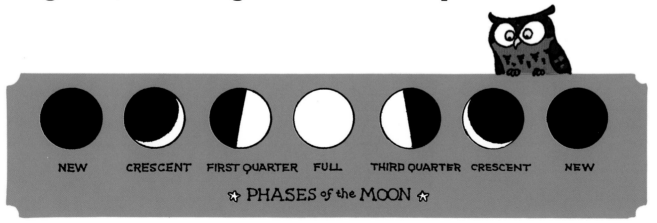

| NEW | CRESCENT | FIRST QUARTER | FULL | THIRD QUARTER | CRESCENT | NEW |

★ PHASES of the MOON ★

You can do your own experiment to show the phases of the moon. You'll need a good flashlight, an orange, a pencil, a marker, and a friend.

Stick the pencil into the orange. Push it in far enough so the orange doesn't fall off.

With the marker draw a line all around the orange. Start and end where the pencil goes into the orange. Make a big X on one half of the orange.

The orange will be the moon, and your head will be the Earth. The flashlight is the sun.

EARTH   MOON   SUN

Hold the orange a bit above your head so that you have to look up to see it. Turn it so that the X is toward you. Have someone on the other side of the orange shine the flashlight on it. Do this in a dark room—the darker the better.

You cannot see the lighted half of the orange. It is a new moon.

Stand on one spot. Turn your body a bit while holding the orange in front of you and a bit above your head. Always keep the X toward you. You will see a small part of the lighted half. It is a crescent moon.

←TURN UNTIL YOU SEE THIS.

Keep turning, and soon you will see more of the lighted half of the orange. It is a first-quarter moon.

Keep the orange above your head and turn some more. Soon you will see all the lighted half of the orange. The moon is full.

Keep turning and you will see less and less of the lighted part of the orange. You will see one quarter of it—the third-quarter moon. Then you'll see a thin crescent. When you have turned all the way around, you have seen all the phases of the orange—the phases of the moon.

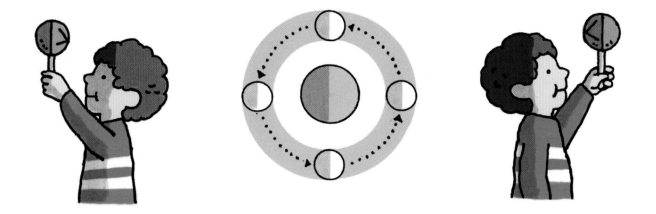

You held the orange so that the X on it was always toward you. That's the way it is with the moon. The same half of it is always toward Earth.

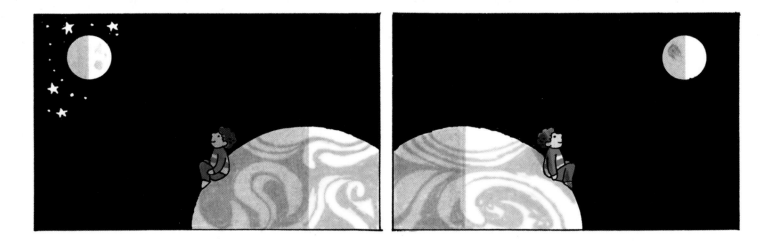

THIS IS THE
SIDE OF THE MOON
YOU CAN SEE
FROM EARTH.

Until spaceships went around the moon, we had never seen the other half of it.

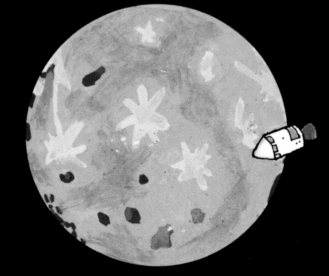

THE OTHER SIDE

Sometimes we see a lot of the part of the moon that is turned toward us, and sometimes only a little of it. The moon grows bigger, and then gets smaller. The moon seems to change. It goes through phases because it goes around Earth.

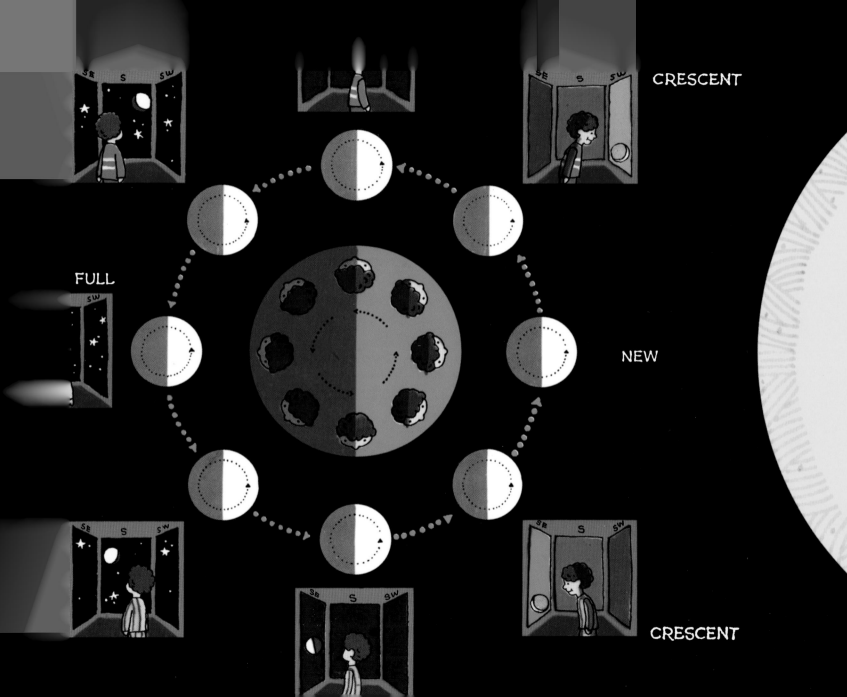

CRESCENT

FULL

NEW

CRESCENT

EARTH   MOON   SUN